THE BOOK THAT DRIPPED BLOOD

BY MICHAEL DAHL
ILLUSTRATED BY BRADFORD KENDALL

Librarian Reviewer
Laurie K. Holland
Media Specialist (National Board Certified), Edina, MN
MA in Elementary Education, Minnesota State University, Mankato

Reading Consultant
Elizabeth Stedem
Educator/Consultant, Colorado Springs, CO
MA in Elementary Education, University of Denver, CO

STONE ARCH BOOKS
Minneapolis   San Diego

Zone Books are published by Stone Arch Books,
1710 Roe Crest Drive,
North Mankato, Minnesota 56003.
www.capstonepub.com

Copyright © 2007 by Stone Arch Books

Library of Congress Cataloging-in-Publication Data
Dahl, Michael.
   The Book That Dripped Blood / by Michael Dahl;
illustrated by Bradford Kendall.
   p. cm. — (Zone Books - Library of Doom)
   Summary: A fur-covered book entitled Claws is loose in
the city, and only the Librarian can stop it from claiming more
victims.
   ISBN-13: 978-1-59889-324-3 (library binding)
   ISBN-10: 1-59889-324-6 (library binding)
   ISBN-13: 978-1-59889-419-6 (paperback)
   ISBN-10: 1-59889-419-6 (paperback)
   1. Books and reading—Fiction. 2. Librarians—Fiction.
3. Fantasy. I. Kendall, Bradford, ill. II. Title.
PZ7.D15134Boo 2007
[Fic]—dc22   2006027530

Art Director: Heather Kindseth
Cover Graphic Designer: Brann Garvey
Interior Graphic Designer: Kay Fraser

Printed in the United States of America in Eau Claire, Wisconsin.
052014
008167R

TABLE OF CONTENTS

 he Library of Doom is the world's largest collection of strange and dangerous books. The Librarian's duty is to keep the books from falling into the hands of those who would use them for evil purposes.

4

CHAPTER 1

THE GOLDEN HINGES

A young man hurries down a dark street. Cuts and bruises cover his face. His left arm is in a sling.

In his right hand, he carries a package tied with **thick rope**.

At the end of the street, he finds what he is looking for. He walks into a small bookstore.

An older man, bent and wrinkled, stands behind a counter.

"Do you buy used books?" asks the young man.

"What do you have?" asks the old man.

The young man throws his package down on the counter.

The old storekeeper unties the thick rope and opens the package.

"Is this made of fur?" asks the old man.

"**Look at the spine,**" says the younger man.

The old man turns the book on its side.

Two yellow hinges hold the book together.

"They're made of gold," says the young man. "How much will you give me for it?"

The old man pulls out a handful of cash and hands it to the young man. The young man turns and runs out the door.

The old man looks closer at the shaggy cover. He brushes the fur aside and reads **Claws.**

A few moments later, a young woman on the street hears a man _screaming_ inside the bookstore.

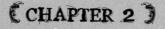

CHAPTER 2

T HE S TOLEN B OOK

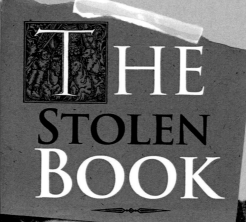

The young woman rushes inside the bookstore.

A pair of legs **stick out** from behind the counter.

The woman hears a man moaning in pain.

"Get it away from me!" says the bookseller.

The woman's eyes follow the direction that the man is pointing.

She sees a 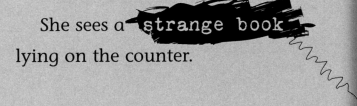 strange book lying on the counter.

She picks up the book.

The gold hinges **gleam**.

"This is beautiful," she says to herself.

—"Help me," moans the bookseller.

The woman clutches the book to her chest, and then she hurries out the door.

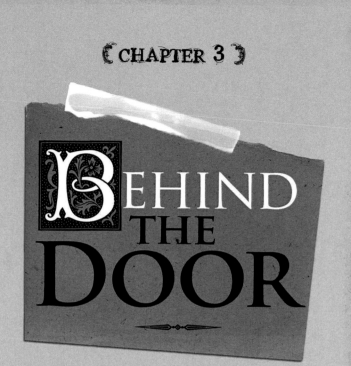

CHAPTER 3

BEHIND THE DOOR

The young woman **rushes** into her apartment building.

The landlord sees her from his door. "You owe me rent," he calls out to her.

She hurries into her apartment and shuts the door behind her.

A few minutes later, the landlord climbs the stairs to the woman's apartment. Her rooms are dark.

The woman is missing.

The landlord sees a dark puddle on the floor. Next to the puddle lies a furry book.

The landlord picks up the book. "Ow!" The man yells and drops the book.

He sees the book slowly open.

The pages fold themselves into
sharp, rounded points.

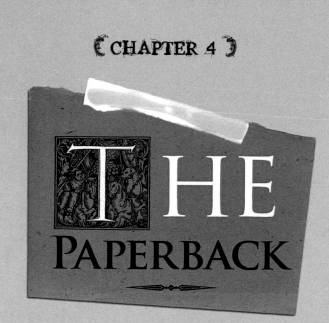

CHAPTER 4

THE PAPERBACK

The landlord backs away from the book on the floor. He bumps into a table. A paperback in his back pocket falls to the floor.

Ink from its pages **oozes** out and covers the floor.

The puddle of ink grows larger.

A tall, dark shape rises from the bubbling ink.

The ink forms into the shape of a man.

It is the Librarian.

He has been waiting inside the pages of the paperback.

He knew that the furry book would come to this apartment building, but he did not know when.

CHAPTER 5

THE COLLECTOR

The book leaps into the air. Its golden hinges open as it flies toward the Librarian's throat.

The Librarian ducks and the book **slams** against a wall.

With another roar, the book
flashes its teeth. It darts across the
floor and grips the Librarian's leg.

The Librarian **screams**.

The landlord is **scared**.
He runs into the hallway and
down the stairs.

Suddenly, the front door of the
building **swings** open.

A young man rushes in.

He is the same man who
sold the **strange** furry book to
the bookseller.

"Where is the book?" the young
man demands.

The landlord points up the stairs.

The Librarian has pulled the
book off his leg. Blood drips
onto his shoe.

He snaps his fingers. A small
blue flame **bursts** from his hand.

The book backs away from
the flame and crouches in a
`dark corner.`

The door bangs open. It is the
young man.

"That is mine," he says, pointing
to the furry book.

The Librarian looks hard at the
man. "`The Collector,`" he mutters.

"Yes," says the man. "And I am here to collect my book."

"That book belongs to the Library of Doom," says the Librarian.

"It needs to be free," says the Collector. "The book is hungry."

"And each time the book feeds," says the Librarian, "the more powerful you become."

The Collector smiles. He pulls another book from his pocket and throws it through a window.

The new book hangs outside
the window and grows larger.

Quickly, the Collector jumps
onto the **floating book**.

The flying book soars away from the apartment building. It disappears into the shadowy city.

"The battle is not over, yet," the Librarian says to himself.

He picks up the landlord's old paperback from the floor. The title reads *The Book That Dripped Blood*.

Then the Librarian sinks back down into the book.

Waiting.

THE END

A PAGE FROM
THE LIBRARY
OF DOOM

RARE and UNUSUAL BOOKS

The world's bestselling book is the Bible, with almost 2.5 billion copies sold since 1815.

According to the Guinness World Records, the longest novel ever written is *In Search of Lost Time* by Marcel Proust.

The world's largest book was made by Michael Hawley of the U.S. in 2003. It weighs more than 130 pounds and uses enough paper to cover a football field.

Some experts say the world's smallest book is an edition of *Chameleon*, by Anton Chekhov. The tiny book has 30 pages and is only a little bigger than a grain of salt!

In 1939, Frank Siebert, a medical student, raised money to buy a rare book on American Indians by selling bottles of his own blood!

ABOUT THE AUTHOR

Michael Dahl is the author of more than 100 books for children and young adults. He has twice won the AEP Distinguished Achievement Award for his nonfiction. His Finnegan Zwake mystery series was chosen by the Agatha Awards to be among the five best mystery books for children in 2002 and 2003. He collects books on poison and graveyards, and lives in a haunted house in Minneapolis, Minnesota.

ABOUT THE ILLUSTRATOR

Bradford Kendall has enjoyed drawing for as long as he can remember. As a boy, he loved to read comic books and watch old monster movies. He graduated from the Rhode Island School of Design with a BFA in Illustration. He has owned his own commercial art business since 1983, and lives in Providence, Rhode Island, with his wife, Leigh, and their two children Lily and Stephen. They also have a cat named Hansel and a dog named Gretel. Sometimes, they all sit together to watch an old monster movie.

GLOSSARY

clutch (KLUTCH)—to hold tightly

mutter (MUH-tur))—to speak in a low voice with your mouth almost closed

snarl (SNARL)—to show your teeth and growl

spine (SPYN)—the edge of a book that holds it together

DISCUSSION QUESTIONS

1. The Collector likes to keep books, not give them away. Why do you think the Collector sold his book to the bookseller at the beginning of the story?

2. Why did the young woman take the book, even though she saw the bookseller had been hurt? What should she have done instead?

3. Do you think it's all right for the Collector to own such a dangerous book? Why or why not? Is it the same thing as having a dangerous pet? What do you think about those kinds of animals? What makes a pet dangerous?

WRITING PROMPTS

1. At the end of the story, the Collector flies off on his book. Where does he go next? Will he give someone else the book named *Claws*? Does the Librarian find him again? Write a short story and describe what the Collector does.

2. Imagine that you have a book as a pet. Your book is not as wild as *Claws*, but still needs to be fed and taken care of. Describe your book. What does it look like? What noises does it make? What does it eat? Where did you get it? Do you ever take it to school?

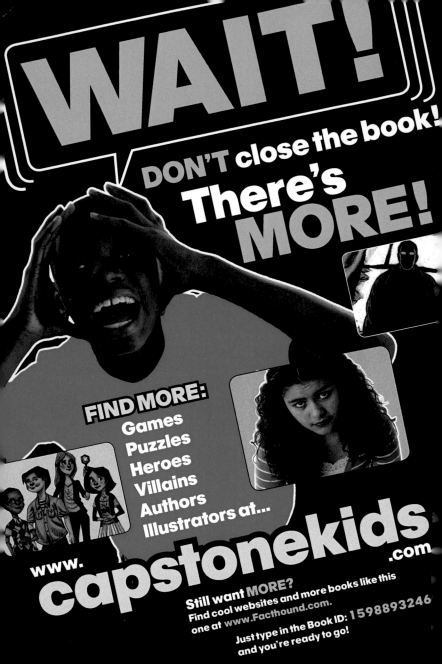